Flowers In December

Omkar Bhatkar

Ukiyoto Publishing

All global publishing rights are held by

Ukiyoto Publishing

Published in 2023

Content Copyright © Omkar Bhatkar
Cover Photograph by Harshvardhan Shetye
ISBN 9789360168445

All rights reserved.
No part of this publication may be reproduced, transmitted, or stored in a retrieval system, in any form by any means, electronic, mechanical, photocopying, recording or otherwise, without the prior permission of the publisher.

The moral rights of the author have been asserted.

This is a work of fiction. Names, characters, businesses, places, events, locales, and incidents are either the products of the author's imagination or used in a fictitious manner. Any resemblance to actual persons, living or dead, or actual events is purely coincidental.

This book is sold subject to the condition that it shall not by way of trade or otherwise, be lent, resold, hired out or otherwise circulated, without the publisher's prior consent, in any form of binding or cover other than that in which it is published.

Dedicated to
Mom, Dad, and Brother

Pratibha Joshi
Sharmila Velaskar Kadne
Archana Bora
Berges Santok
Viraj Dey
Amit Valmiki
Carlos Gonzalvo Garralaga

Characters

Aparajita

Aparajita settled in Sweden working at the Indian Consulate where lives a very comfortable life. She has minimized her worries and lives a life of a pattern where not many new things happen and each day is like another. She has been staying away from India and her two daughters for almost a decade now and talks to them on the phone occasionally.

William

William (40 - 45 years) moved to Sweden at the age of 35 and has been working there as a finance analyst for the last few years. He is a spinster who lives a meticulous life, where he measures his choices cautiously and speaks only after giving it a thought. William is aware of the ephemeral nature of life and yet he seeks something everlasting.

Hyacintha

Hyacintha (21-26 years) likes being with people, she can spend time even with strangers but it takes her efforts to talk to her mother Aparajita. Hyacintha is an independent girl and works as a copyeditor for a publishing house. Christmas excites her be it sweets preparation or decorating the house, putting up the tree and the manger, she loves it all.

Kunal

Kunal (21-26 years) is a dear friend of Hyacintha who lives for the present unconcerned about the future and makes the most of the present moment. He isn't aware of his life's goals; he only knows that he can make people happy and he plays the acoustic guitar well. Kunal is a romantic at heart and still preserves the childishness in him.

Hazel

Hazel (28-30 years) is a microbiologist by profession married to a businessman and living happily with two children and her in-laws. Her in-laws are traditional and disciplined and believe in upholding traditions of the family be it any kind of events. Hazel puts her family before her profession and is somehow striking a balance but she knows within her heart that it's an imbalance, her time maximum time is spent running the family. In spite of it, she has a smile and doesn't ever feel that she is sacrificing anything for anything. She is content and her happiness draws from keeping her family happy,

The play premiered in Mumbai at St. Andrew's Centre for Philosophy and Performing Arts in December 2023, Directed by Dr. Omkar Bhatkar.

The Characters were essayed by the following actors:

William - Amit Rai

Aparajita - Meeta Bagwe

Hyacintha - Zahra Patka

Kunal - Mohit Raghuvanshi

Hazel - Ria Sadhwani

Writer-Director Note

Flowers in December is a play written to talk about the spoken and the unspoken in families. On the outside, we all try to respect and care for each other, very often we create an ever-embracing smiling familial image of ourselves. How difficult is it to carry this image? Flowers in December is a play where the 'unsaid' in the relationships is given an opportunity to be 'said' and what happens when the unspoken is spoken. How does the 'unspoken' affect relationships? What happens when a daughter who has repressed her real feelings for her mother speaks them out? What happens when a mother expresses her feelings never expressed? Who is the victim and who is the perpetrator? The play is an attempt to look at life's fragilities and how life doesn't prepare us for this thing called 'life'. In the backdrop of December, the play tries to look into our interior feelings. Throughout, the last scene of the play we see characters speaking what's in their heart but in real end up saying something else but only in the end when the mist is cleared, armours of self-defence are put down, we see people as they are fragile creatures' victims of time/life.

The flowers at the door remain a mystery. The readers/ audience/and director/ actors are free to interpret the sender of the flowers for Aparajita.

The song 'Walk in the Spring Rain' is penned by Don Black from the film A Walk in the Spring Rain (1970). The character Kunal can create a cover song for it and sing it.

The Poem 'The Way the Cookie Crumbles' is penned by Gretchen Ferro.

The play if staged can be accompanied by lilting acoustic guitar (Live or pre-recorded) for emotional sequences and blackouts.

For public performances and staging of the play kindly get in touch on

metamorphosistheatreinc@gmail.com

Contents

Scene I	1
Scene II	5
Scene III	7
Scene IV	12
Scene V	15
Scene VI	21
About the Author	*32*

Scene I

Advent Sunday

William and Aparajita conversing in a cafe or Aparajita's home on a Sunday morning, sipping their coffee.

William : You want to meet her?

Aparajita : I don't know.

William : Why are you being so tough on yourself?

Aparajita : I don't know William, why am I doing this to myself, to us?

William : When was the last time you spent your Christmas with her?

Aparajita : It's hard, I can't even remember | Must be about seven years ago

William : But why are you thinking now? You've already spoken to Hazel that you're coming.

Aparajita : I've spoken to Hazel and it's not here that I'm worried about.

William : It's Hyacintha?

Aparajita : It's always been something about her, between us that I have never been able to reckon.

William : Are you regretting your decision of going to spend Christmas with them?

Aparajita : I don't even understand, what is it that I regret.

William : I'm aware of some of the incidents that you have shared about you and Hyacintha, but somewhere they need to be resolved or at least be spoken instead of keeping it in hiding under a blanket as if everything is all right. Most people go on living their lives, hiding it all under the blanket of their covered hearts, never unveiling what's inside. But that only leads to living incomplete moments. Yes, we all have regrets and most of us know that those regrets, as excruciating as they can be, are the things that help us lead improved lives.

William : Do you regret something, Aparajita? Then go and talk it out. Regrets keep forever floating to the surface… they never let us rest peacefully. Whenever it's about Hyacintha, you're restless, worried and unsure

Aparajita : Yes, exactly. Whenever it's about Hyacintha, I just feel small. In her greatness of age and innocence, I'm reduced to my pettiness. And I start feeling regretful.

William : Then, that's good, at least to feel regret. At least, you have not become oblivious to feelings, at least you are not unconcerned. Regrets keep floating awaiting our attention. You have to do something with them.

Aparajita : What do I do with regret? And I don't even know if I'm regretful because I don't feel it unless I see Hyacintha. She is a constant reminder of anguish.

William : And you've never spoken about this to her?

Aparajita : How does one talk about anguish and pain between a daughter and mother? Were we ever trained for this in our life? When we give birth to our children, we are barely 28 years to 30 years old. How much of life do we understand ourselves, how much of ourselves do we know when we are 30? And to bring a new child into a world at such an age when we hardly understand anything? How do I tell my daughter whom to love and whom not to? How do I tell her that the love between me and her father vanished soon after she was born? How do we tell our children how capable are they to understand these fragilities at their own tender age?

William : Seek forgiveness

Aparajita : from her?

William : No, from yourself

William : Forgive yourself, Aparajita. Talk to yourself and see what you can do to forgive yourself. Do that and then try to help rehabilitate the world with whatever is possible through your actions.

Aparajita : How do I do that William?

William : You're already doing that? Don't you remember what you were doing in Drottninggatan? It is our actions that make the world a measurably better place than it is. Your bag is a testimony to that, just that it doesn't look like a Santa Claus sack and I'm assuming you're going to fill it with time and probably the Santa from Sweden would climb down the chimney in Mumbai.

Aparajita : There are no chimneys in Mumbai
(laughs)

Aparajita : How do you make it so simple William?

William : Let me tell you a simple way, whenever I'm confused and lost and don't know what to do, I ask myself, what would you do right now if you learned that you were going to die in ten minutes? Would I race upstairs and light that Marlboro I've been hiding in the drawer since the Ford administration? Would I waltz into your boss's office and present him with a detailed description of his personal defects? Would I drive out to that Pizza House near Nordby and order an ultra-thin multigrain, medium rare, with an extra side of the really *bad* cholesterol?

Scene II

Pretensions

The scene unveils on the stage with the play of light, where Aparajita is on the left side of the stage and Hyacintha is on the right side. Whenever they speak the light brightens and fades with falling dialogue. Both are addressing the audience or speaking to themselves.

Hyacintha : I don't know what am I going to do. How am I going to be in front of her? I've no clue out of nowhere, how is she leaving Sweden which she hasn't in the last seven years. And above all, I've no idea why has she chosen this Christmas season.

Aparajita : I know she would be as clueless as me, maybe surprised, no – no surprise actually shocked, I just hope my arrival won't spoil her plans.

Hyacintha : It's Christmas, how do I spend it with my mother whom I haven't seen for the last seven years, and what about those friends whom I've known for a long?

Aparajita : I don't want to be a bother.

Hyacintha : She will bother me and all of us. Maybe, I will have to rethink who is coming over and whom should I invite in front of her.

Aparajita : Will I have to pretend?

Hyacintha : I will have to wear a mask this Christmas.

Aparajita and Hyacintha *(together)* : So, we will pretend.

Scene III

The Meet

The doorbell rings and Hyacintha opens the door. Outside the door, flowers are left with the name Aparajita. Aparajita picks them and Hyacintha opens the door. Aparajita hugs her daughter after ages. They smile and look at each other with conviction knowing in their hearts that they are unsure of what is to follow. Aparajita's suitcase is massive and Hyacintha helps her carry that. Aparajita takes a few moments to notice her daughter's neatness in keeping the house immaculate and orderly. Aparajita finds the empty vase on the table and says

Aparajita : Someone has left these flowers, the note only says my name, but doesn't mention from whom.

Aparajita hums a song and arranges them in a vase

Hyacintha offers Aparajita a glass of water and goes to put the suitcase at one side of the wall. While she picks up the suitcase, she says.

Hyacintha *(hesitantly)* : Mom, for how long will you be?

Interior thought of Aparajita while addressing the audience. Everyone on the stage freezes except the person speaking their interior thoughts. Lights dim in the other sections of the stage

Aparajita : Is she asking me when will I leave?

Interior thought of Hyacintha said while addressing the audience. Everyone on the stage freezes except the person speaking their interior thoughts. Lights dim in the other sections of the stage

Hyacintha : Her big bag, constantly reminds me of the heavy weight of life and that's how long it's going to be, but how long do I need to know so that I'm prepared in my head?

Aparajita responds to Hyacintha

Aparajita : I 've booked my tickets for 6th January.

Hyacintha : I didn't mean to ask you that way, but you're leaving that early.

Aparajita : Can't be longer than that, you too have your life. How long can I stay and bother you?

Hyacintha : No, don't say that. I've never made you feel like that.

Aparajita : Then, why did you ask that when am I leaving?

Hyacintha : I'm sorry, I didn't mean it that way, the big bag is the cause of this question.

Aparajita : oh, it's the big bag. Didn't know a bag that doesn't even belong to me could create such misunderstandings.

Aparajita : It's all yours and Hazels

Hyacintha : Then why didn't you say that first?

Aparajita : Because it didn't strike me that my daughter would be condemned to believe that I'm staying for longer than necessary just because of a Santa's bag.

Hyacintha : I'm sorry again.

Aparajita : It doesn't matter, it's all right.

Hyacintha : And why haven't you given me these gifts?

Aparajita : Because it's not Christmas yet and I was hoping that we could open it when Hazel is here.

Hyacintha : Mom, have you ever thought of me before Hazel anytime? (tearfully)

Hyacintha : I'm seriously asking Mom, have you ever thought of me before Hazel?

Hyacintha : It's always Hazel. Whether it's buying a bag from Sangam, we will buy the polka-dotted one because Hazel likes them. We will go to Dona Paula because Hazel likes it there, but not to the sweet water lake at Arambol. Why is it always about Hazel? You said you loved both of us equally, but that's not true because you loved her more than me.

Aparajita : I'm sorry for not being honest with you, we parents are often so burdened with the falsities that we just can't speak the truth. Sometimes, I feel there should be a curriculum for parenting and one of its chapters should deal with being honest with siblings. It wouldn't have been difficult to say that, yes, Hazel was closer to my heart. Not that you were distant, but somewhere I was more attached to her as my daughter, and probably even love more, but how can a parent say that they love one child more than the other? Can we? Can we say that?

The burden of societal norms made it easier to be dishonest than to truly say what we feel. But why I love her more is a wrong question, love can't be measured in how much more and less, only that I was deeply attached to her and that could be possible because she was my only hope and my only friend when the world was collapsing for me.

Dad and I would often fight and the 10 x 10 room would be suffocating to breathe with the smoke of anguish. I would step out take Hazel with me, and stand at the bus stop waiting for No 100. Would climb in that double-decker bus and go and sit right on the top in the front seat. The bus would go from Santacruz to Colaba back and forth, and whenever I felt I had cried enough, I would come home. Hazel was only six then, I still don't know what she understood then. that, why was her mother crying? I still don't know if she knows now. But she would comprehend that there is immense pain, pain incapable of being articulated, pain impossible to be put into words, flowing out of warm eyes, in the form of tears. Those tears also left me, but Hazel was beside holding my hands when no one was there.

Aparajita gradually opens the suitcase

Hyacintha : I've asked a friend to come tomorrow to help me with marzipan. Hope you don't mind.

Aparajita : I didn't know you make Christmas sweets too.

Hyacintha : I learned them gradually, not all of them, just the marzipan, guava cheese, kalkals, cocoa rocks, and plum cake, my cookies always crumble, so I don't try anymore.

Aparajita : But you never took interest in the sweets when I made them.

Hyacintha : *(smiles in agreement)*

Blackout

Scene IV

Cookie that Crumbles

Light fades out with a spotlight on Hyacintha. Hyacintha presents her elocution piece as a memory/flashback. She recites in the tone of an adolescent.

Hyacintha :

Rarely called by my own name,

I am a proud recipient of hand-me-downs, toys, clothes, mobiles, etc.

I've heard "I am older and smarter than you" more times than I can count.

I grew up believing that I was either adopted or worse I was found in a dustbin...

Yes, I am the treasured, younger sister. Often branded the spoilt lot, but you know what they say "Power comes with a price for everyone pesters me to be like my older sister Hazel.

She has everything, smartness, coolness, cuteness, and to add a big juicy cherry Hazel tops the Board Exams this year. Please don't get me wrong. I am super happy for my sister,

but

"why do I have to be like her?."

Hearing Grandma call out to me I scramble into her room. It was a sight to behold.

Dressed in Dad's jacket, his Raybans, and my Converse shoes Grandma starts rapping.

"My granddaughter Hazel is the school topper. Yo! Hazel Grandma's so proud of you. This is for my Instagram reel cookie. Stop gawking. Come hold the phone in seascape mode."

Err Grandma you mean landscape mode and why am I always your personal selfie stick? Why not Hazel? Because you look like a stick.

Idli, dosa, upma, poha nothing you eat.

Hazel eats everything that's why she looks like Katrina Kaif.....and Grandma I look like? "You, you are my Mowgli".

I shake my head in despair.

Suddenly..."Nonoo..How are we Indians going to qualify for the World Cup?" Yells my football crazy Dad jumping from his couch potato position. Holding my scrawny shoulders, he said" Cookie, I shall teach you to play football like Ronaldo."

"Dad but I don't really like to play football," I say meekly.

"Nonsense if Hazel can do it, so can you. Now please put my mobile to charge".

Ask Hazel to do it, Dad. If I can do it so, can she.

She paints her nails and is on the phone all day.

But we seconds are designated errand runners so I pick up the phone only to bump into Mom

"Again with the mobile? You have exams. Hazel would never touch the phone when she had to study. You saw the outcome. Follow her example Cookie"

Finally, this cookie crumbled. With tears in my eyes and hands clenched into fists,

I whispered

"Hazel's great at a lot of things, but I'm a different person, and sometimes it hurts when you compare me to her. I am me, special and unique. She is the sun but I may be the moon and will shine at my own time. Could you help me shine without making it all about her?

Can you please stop your cookie from crumbling?

Light's turn to normal, and Hyacintha addresses the audience saying

Hyacintha : This was the elocution piece that I had chosen but the teacher asked me to pick something by Roald Dahl and I only ended up preparing this piece just for myself.

Scene V

Arts

Kunal is already in the living room with Hyacintha going in and out of the kitchen which is the part of the living room separated by a thin bead curtain.

Hyacintha : Just be a little easy, don't get over-excited, and talk too much.

Hyacintha : Already you're overdoing it by bringing these flowers…..

Kunal : I talk too much, really. And flowers are overdoing, just because you're not getting them, btw I didn't get them……

Hyacintha : There she comes….. *(Says softly)*

Aparaijta walks in from her room

Kunal : Hi.

Aparajita : Hello, I'm Aparajita.

(Aparajita admires the carnations brought by Kunal and reads the note on it)

Kunal : Yes, I've heard a lot from Hyacintha about you.

Aparajita : I hope good things,

Aparajita : like….. like what…… say a few…..

Kunal : aaaaaaa

Aparajita : like what...... say a few......

Hyacintha : It's ok. Kunal is a little shy person, doesn't talk much

Kunal : No, I'm not shy. Of course, I can make conversations.

Aparajita : like

Kunal : like on the Arts.

Aparajita : Arts, I see.

Hyacintha : I'm getting some milkmaid, Kunal why don't you come in ... the kitchen table would be more comfortable (*unsurely*)

Kunal : No, no, I'm fine here and even I can talk about the arts.

Hyacintha : Alright, suit yourself

Kunal : aauuuuuu......... wasn't that a bit mean.

Aparajita : That's ok, you know Hyacintha well.

Kunal : hmmm.... So, I've heard you used to act in plays, that's quite an artist. Do you still act there?

Interior thought of Hyacintha said while addressing the audience. Everyone on the stage freezes except the person speaking their interior thoughts. Lights dim in the other sections of the stage, Aparajita and Kunal frozen.

Hyacintha : She is always acting, even now. Hello, I'm Aparajita. Why does she do this? Why wouldn't dad be angry with all this? Of course, he didn't like this. Who would like it?

Interior thoughts are over. Light's return to normal. Frozen characters move to normalcy.

Aparajita : What do you think of art like our reasons for creating art?

Kunal : I think art is solace. Art has the ability to save us, in so many different ways. It can act as a point of salvation because it has the potential to put beauty back into the world.

Kunal : I have heard your interview which aired on the Radio then.

Aparajita : Really, why did you hear it?

Kunal : Why wouldn't I, it's an honor to meet you. You have played Lysistrata, Penelope, and even the Virgin Mary, whom else have I met with such a large body of work in person?

Aparajita : Thank you, you're really polite and kind.

Kunal : If you don't mind, can you please elaborate on why do you say art is reconciliation in that interview of yours?

Aparajita : Art as reconciliation. I feel we are fragile creatures rather than part of a puppet show unaware of the puppeteer's intentions and therefore we move to the tunes of the one who is pulling the strings. While we are part of this game, this world we think we are free, we can choose. But we are wrong, we aren't totally free and there are not infinite choices, but limited ones from which we are doomed to choose. The option of not choosing doesn't exist. So, in the choices, we make from our limited understanding of life, we are bound to make some mistakes. Mistakes remain as mistakes as we don't correct them. With time they harden and become a part of us. This hardening makes us heavy and we are burdened by the weight of suffering gradually alienating us from those around us. Art is a way of mitigating the pain as it helps in reconciling our decisions, and our choices, and somewhere tries to lighten us by loosening the burden of suffering in life.

Kunal : Wow ……. Art as reconciliation *(smile)*

Aparajita : What do you do in the arts?

Kunal : I'm not an artist or something, I'm just an amateur poet.

Aparajita : You say 'amateur' as if it isn't a good thing.

Kunal : Yeah, because I'm average, just an amateur poet.

Aparajita : Do you know 'Amateur' comes from the Latin word 'amare', which means to love. To do things for the love of it."

Kunal : (applauds)

Interior thought of Hyacintha said while addressing the audience.

Hyacintha : How does she do it? Always, always, she, does it? But not this time, I can't let it happen this time............

Can I just barge in and tell him to get out right now?

Hyacintha says the following while walking from the kitchen to the living room, talking to both of them.

Hyacintha : That's it enough of it, Kunal please go home, I need to talk to her.

Blackout

Light's return to normal, and Hyacintha is in the kitchen. Interior thought of Hyacintha said while addressing the audience. Everyone on the stage freezes except the person speaking their interior thoughts. Lights dim in the other sections of the stage, Aparajita and Kunal frozen.

Hyacintha : What do I do? How can I ask him to leave, that's not fair. What would he think?

Interior thoughts are over. Light's return to normal. Frozen characters move to normalcy.

Aparajita : Do you also recite your poems with the guitar?

Kunal : No, not really. Not at least in front of you.

Aparajita : Of course, you can.

Kunal : I'm not carrying my poems….. but I can try singing a song.

Aparajita : that would be great too as long as you help her finish the marzipan today *(smiles)*

Kunal : *(Kunal sings 'A Walk in the Spring Rain'….)*

Hyacintha : *(walks in)*

: Can we please stop this? Why the hell have you come? What do you want now? Don't you have amateur poets in Sweden? You have come all the way from Sweden to receive carnations from a young boy holding a guitar and singing a song for you from a lousy film of Ingrid Bergman, where also eventually she has to go back to her conventional life with her husband. Don't you reckon the closing of the film……..

Blackout

Lights return to normalcy. The singing

continues……..Aparajita and Kunal while singing 'A Walk in the Spring Rain' walk into the kitchen during the last stanza, Hyacintha reluctantly smiles

Blackout

Scene VI

Reconciliation

Another Day in the living room. Hyacintha takes out the raisins soaked in rum for baking the cake and that's when Aparjita walks in……..

Interior thought of Hyacintha said while addressing the audience. Everyone on the stage freezes except the person speaking their interior thoughts. Lights dim in the other sections of the stage, Aparajita and Kunal freeze.

Interior thoughts are over. Light's return to normal. Frozen characters move to normal

Aparajita : You didn't call Kunal today to help you.

Interior thought of Hyacintha said while addressing the audience. Aparajita freezes and Hyacintha shares her interior thoughts with the audience. Lights dim in the other sections of the stage.

Hyacintha : She even has the audacity to ask me.

Interior thoughts are over. Light's return to normal. Frozen Aparajita moves to normalcy

Hyacintha : No, it was manageable. Didn't want to bother him.

Aparajita : Is something bothering you Hyacintha?

They both remain silent and eventually, Aparajita says in a concerned manner.

Aparajita : You can tell me, please. We can talk.

Hyacintha : What do we talk about Mom? I just don't know how to talk. Didn't we forget to talk to each other after Dad left?

Aparajita : You mean to say when your dad and I separated?

Hyacintha : Yeah, separated, left.

Aparajita : No, it's not the same thing. He didn't leave, and we mutually decided to separate.

Hyacintha : whatever, I don't wish to talk about it.

Aparajita : and why?

Hyacintha : Mom, can we just forget it? Can we just spend this Christmas pretending that nothing has happened and let it go?

Aparajita : Aren't you pretending from the time I've come, is it helping? If the mask is still not helping, we might as be ourselves.

Hyacintha : Mom, you are the way you are.

Aparajita : So is it you, who is wearing a mask?

They both remain silent for a moment.

Aparajita : Take it off Hyacintha, let me also see my daughter without the mask.

Hyacintha : would you have the courage to see, Mom? *(Short pause and rethinking of the thought)* Well, actually you would, where has anything affected you so much?

Aparajita : Just because I don't show my scars, doesn't mean that it doesn't exist.

Hyacintha : Where are your scars Mumma, why don't you show them and create more drama.

Aparajita : So, you call all this drama? And it's me who creates drama?

Hyacintha : What did Dad do to you, did he beat you up, did he hit you?

Aparajita : do you think physical beating is the only form of violence in a marriage?

Silence

The doorbell rings, and Hyacintha goes to the door to open it. Kunal enters

Kunal : I called you so many times, but you didn't pick up. I even sent you the WhatsApp pics but seems like you have forgotten about your phone. What a transformation just because the mother is back from Sweden, madam has forgotten about everything else.

Kunal : These are for you *(handing Aparajita a bouquet)*

Kunal : I tried my best to get the snowball lights which were available last week, but there are nowhere in Crawford. We should have picked it up last week, I was telling you but you insisted on buying later. Anyway, I've to go to these Santa ones.

He starts putting the light decoration on the door

Kunal : Why are you so quiet?

Aparajita : Hello! Kunal

Kunal : Hi,

Aparajita : you had gone to Crawford.

Kunal : Yeah, Hyacintha wanted me to pick up some lights and packaging boxes.

Hyacintha : You didn't get small paper stars.

Kunal : I don't know what's wrong with these people. They are selling for 2400/- small six-paper stars.

Hyacintha : that's Rs 400/- for each

Aparajita : When did paper stars become so expensive?

Kunal : Post-pandemic everything is drastically changed.

Kunal : Hyacintha, are you ok!

Hyacintha : yeah, just a bit headache.

Kunal : Always overthinking!

Hyacintha : Why would you say that....

Kunal : Because you always estimate more than necessary, always in the future.

Hyacintha : Because I like to be prepared for the future so that things don't go topsy turvy.

Kunal : Hyacintha, however hard and well you plan. There is no assurance that things will turn out like you have planned. You know that, don't you? Then why live for the future?

Kunal : What do you think of sacrificing the present for the future? About saving the acorns for the winter, what if you are not even there to have them? What if it's not that bad winter? But in preparing for winter, one loses the beauty of being in the spring and gathering some blossoms.

Aparajita : I have thought about the future, one can't ignore what will come but not at the cost of what is there. We never know what will be and where will be after 10 years. Will we even be the same person or would we have changed? If the person you will be in 10 years — the person for whom you plan your life now by working toward career goals and putting money aside in retirement plans — is invariably different from the person you are today, what makes that future person "you"? What makes them worthy of your present self's sacrifices and considerations?

Hyacintha : This is why probably; you are where you are now.

Aparajita : What do you mean by that Hyacintha?

Hyacintha : I don't know mom, it's difficult to articulate but you have just been too wise. Not everyone reaches there easily.

Aparajita : I've not reached there easily Hyacintha. I too have paid the price for the same. Everything around as much as fulfilling is also hurtful. Wisdom comes when we have lived through pain. Wisdom is actually being used by life; hurt by life, driven and goaded by life, replenished and overjoyed with life, fighting for life's sake. That is real wisdom. In the undergoing, a large part of it is pain. Many just choose not to go through pain. But beauty also emerges from pain, pain is not only ugly but also the source of wisdom, of growth.

Kunal : Grandpa was wise, not as wise as mom or dad. There was something about him, possibly life, the war, or endurance that made him what he was.

I was sleeping on my bed with Rohit sleeping next to me in our bedroom, it was early morning. The door was open. He came, as usual, to wake me up. In a half-asleep state, I realized it was him entering the room. I didn't move with the sheet covering our unclad selves up to the chest, he saw us resting in the cocoon. I pretended I was asleep, but I was watching him with half-closed eyes. He stood at the bed for a brief moment and calmly moved to my window to water the plants like every morning and left the room as it was, just like before.

Something within me and grandpa changed that morning, like the opening of a flower, it was gentle and so subtle that neither of us realized it. Something changed and yet it remained unchanged.

He was really wise. Where did he bring that wisdom from? Did it come from life, pain, war, endurance, or simply the love of a grandson?

Aparajita : Hope, the hope of a grandson's joy. The concern for other's joy brings joy to us. To place our hope in another person is to instantly entwine destinies, linking self and others in a tender and tenacious recognition of interdependence. All love is a form of hope. All hope is the work of absolute sincerity, which is the emblem of being fully human.

Hyacintha : You think your mom and dad lacked that love?

Aparajita : Maybe they didn't lack love but like all of us are fragile creatures of time who are still giving birth to themselves, still being born.

Aparajita : Birth is not a one-time activity. We are physically born one day that's our birthdate.... as infants we are dependent. Before birth, we cannot perceive things outside and are fully dependent on the womb of the mother to nourish us. Once born, we learn, we recognize things, and we learn to understand but we don't fully understand. We learn to reason, to figure out what we like and what we don't. We develop reasoning and examining logically and we develop a sense of identity.

When someone enters our life, and if we allow ourselves, we experience a new side, a new birth. When they leave, we experience something beyond, something unknown. People give birth to us each time. Birth then, in the conventional meaning of the word, is only the beginning of birth in the broader sense. The whole life of the individual is nothing but the process of giving birth to themself; indeed, we should be fully born, when we die — although it is the tragic fate of most individuals to die before they are born.

Aparajita's words move Kunal to speak the unspoken, He is moved emotionally and say's

Kunal : Mom said she only came to understand a bit of her life when she was 45 but then she said it was too late. She died early, and on her death bed she asked me to re-read a passage every day, possibly she was dying and couldn't remember, or possibly she wanted to relive life through this passage penned by Kalyn RoseAnne

Hazel walks in while all of them are talking, only Hyacintha is aware of her arrival as she was facing the door. Aparajita and Kunal are lost in the moment and facing away from the door, oblivious to the presence of Hazel behind. Hazel recognizes the emotionally charged atmosphere and makes keeps standing solemnly watching over them talking. Kunal recites the passage that he read umpteen times in heavy emotional tone.

Kunal : "Sometimes you're 23 and standing in the kitchen of your house making breakfast and brewing coffee and listening to music that for some reason is really getting to your heart. You're just standing there thinking about going to work and picking up your dry cleaning. And also, more exciting things like books you're reading, and trips you plan on taking, and relationships that are springing into existence. Or fading from your memory, which is far less exciting. And suddenly you just don't feel at home in your skin or in your house and you just want home but 'Moms' probably wouldn't feel like home anymore either. There used to be the comfort of a number in your phone and ears that listened to every day and arms that were never for anyone else. But just to calm you down when you start feeling trapped in a five-minute period where nostalgia is too much and thoughts of this person you are feel foreign. When you realize that you'll never be this young again but this is the first time you've ever been this old. When you can't remember how you got from sixteen to here and all the same feel like sixteen is just as much of a stranger to you now. The song is over. The coffee's done. You're going to breathe in and out. You're going to be fine in about five minutes."

Kunal : I judged her, I judged her so often. We are such miserable products of patriarchy. She was so lonely, and I still judged her……..all that she wanted was someone to talk to, to be there……………

Kunal bursts into tears and Aparajita holds him in her arms. Hyacintha moves closer to them, hugging and speaks

Hyacintha : Why do people have to be this lonely? What's the point of it all? Millions of people in this world, all of them yearning, looking to others to satisfy them, yet isolating themselves. Why? Was the earth put here just to nourish human loneliness?"

Aparajita : That's how you live: you cry, you ache, you hurt, you can't breathe. That's how you move forward, by feeling it all.

Hazel says from behind while the three of them are sitting hugging

Hazel : "Look at the stars.

They all look at her and give a bright smile,

Hazel : "Look at the stars. It won't fix the economy. It won't stop wars. It won't give you flat abs, even help you figure out your relationship and what you want to do with your life. But it's important. It helps you remember that you and your problems are both infinitesimally small and conversely, that you are a piece of an amazing and vast universe."

All we can do is hope and be concerned for others' joy and love. What else can we do, like these flowers in December that bloom in the wild, whether someone sees them or not, they bloom even in times of adversity!

The intensely emotional evening turns a bit light.

Kunal : Just like these wild December flowers, when you look at the flower you cannot help but glimpse the meaning of life.

Aparajita : But. you don't need to bring them every time. *(laughingly)*

Kunal : I didn't bring them; they were at the door outside like last time. I just brought them in.

They all smile and hug at each other. In the background, a Christmas song can be played. Hazel has brought some gifts for all of them. Aparajita opens her suitcase and hands over the gifts she has brought for Hazel and Hyacintha. Kunal can also play a Christmas song on his guitar in the end.

Curtain

In the depths of winter, I finally learned that within me there lay an invincible summer.

- *Albert Camus*

About the Author

Omkar Bhatkar

Dr. Omkar Bhatkar is a Sociologist with a doctoral thesis concerned with Proxemics and Social Ecology. He has been a visiting professor for a decade now teaching Film Theory, Culture Studies, and Gender Studies. He has also served as a faculty for the London School of Economics International Programmes in Sociology.

He is the Co-Founder and Head of the eclectic 'St. Andrew's Centre for Philosophy and Performing Arts', which constantly strives to bridge art and academics. Dr. Omkar Bhatkar runs his own theatre group known as Metamorphosis Theatre Inc. His works largely focus on Poetry in Motion,

Existentialist Themes, and Contemporary French Plays in Translation. He has written and directed more than twenty plays, several of which have been performed at Art and Theatre Festivals. In collaboration with Alliance Française de Bombay, he has directed several Contemporary French Plays in English. He is also a Stage Critic and reviews plays. Dr. Bhatkar's play 'Blue Storm' was selected at the Asia Playwrights Theatre Festival 2021 held in South Korea. 'Blue Storm' was also an invitation play at the International Women's Theatre Festival 2021 held in Incheon, South Korea.

Though he is grounded in theatre, he also explores the world of films. As a filmmaker, he has written and directed independent feature films like Perhaps Tea, The Farewell Band, Testament of Emily, and also a poetic documentary titled 'Painted Hymns: The Chapels of Santa Monica'

He is a tormented thalassophile who finds solace by drowning in the depths of poetry and spends his waking life painting, reading, writing, and engaging in conversations over black tea.

www.ingramcontent.com/pod-product-compliance
Lightning Source LLC
LaVergne TN
LVHW041641070526
838199LV00053B/3494